Run, Bean, Run!

'Run, Bean, Run!'
An original concept by Amanda Brandon
© Amanda Brandon 2021

Illustrated by Camilla Galindo

Published by MAVERICK ARTS PUBLISHING LTD

Studio 11, City Business Centre, 6 Brighton Road,

Horsham, West Sussex, RH13 5BB

© Maverick Arts Publishing Limited November 2021

+44 (0)1403 256941

A CIP catalogue record for this book is available at the British Library.

ISBN 978-1-84886-827-4

www.maverickbooks.co.uk

Green

This book is rated as: Green Band (Guided Reading)
It follows the requirements for Phase 5 phonics.
Most words are decodable, and any non-decodable words are familiar,
supported by the context and/or represented in the artwork.

Run, Bean, Run!

by Amanda Brandon

illustrated by
Camilla Galindo

The sun shines bright. The rain falls.

Little Bean grows and grows until...

...he is picked.

Gran puts a big pot on the stove.

She stirs it. It looks hot.

"Time to go!" Bean yells.

He gets up and runs away.

"Run, Bean, run!"

cheer the peas in a dish.

Bean runs into the garden and hides...

...but Grandad digs in the mud.

"Run, Bean, run!" the slimy snails cheer.

Bean runs into a hole and hides.

It is dark...

...but Rabbit sniffs and tries to catch him.

"Run, Bean, run!" the pink worms

wiggle and cheer.

Bean runs up behind some rocks and hides...

...but there are lots of ants.

They make a long line and pull Bean away.

"Run, Bean, run!" cheers Blackbird in
the sky.

Bean shakes free and runs again.

But Bean huffs and puffs.

He is worn out.

He runs on and on until...

...he finds a new place to hide.

"This looks good," he puffs. "Hooray!

It is hidden from people, rabbits and ants."

Bean climbs in and falls asleep.

One day, the sun shines bright.

Gran starts to pick the beans.

Blackbird calls, "Run, Bean, run!"

But today Gran cannot see Bean.

He is happy and safe in...

...a pot with the flowers.

Quiz

1. What does Bean yell when he runs away?
a) "Time to hop!"
b) "Let's run!"
c) "Time to go!"

2. Who digs in the mud?
a) Gran
b) Grandad
c) Bean

3. Who finds Bean in the hole?
a) Blackbird
b) Gran
c) Rabbit

4. Blackbird calls, "___ ___ ___!"
a) Run, Bean, run
b) Run, Rabbit, run
c) Fly, Bean, fly

5. Where is Bean safe?
a) In a hole
b) A pot with the flowers
c) Behind some rocks

Turn over for answers

Book Bands for Guided Reading

The Institute of Education book banding system is a scale of colours that reflects the various levels of reading difficulty. The bands are assigned by taking into account the content, the language style, the layout and phonics. Word, phrase and sentence level work is also taken into consideration.

Maverick Early Readers are a bright, attractive range of books covering the pink to white bands. All of these books have been book banded for guided reading to the industry standard and edited by a leading educational consultant.

Pink
Red
Yellow
Blue
Green
Orange
Turquoise
Purple
Gold
White

To view the whole Maverick Readers scheme, visit our website at
www.maverickearlyreaders.com

Or scan the QR code above to view our scheme instantly!

Quiz Answers: 1c, 2b, 3c, 4a, 5b